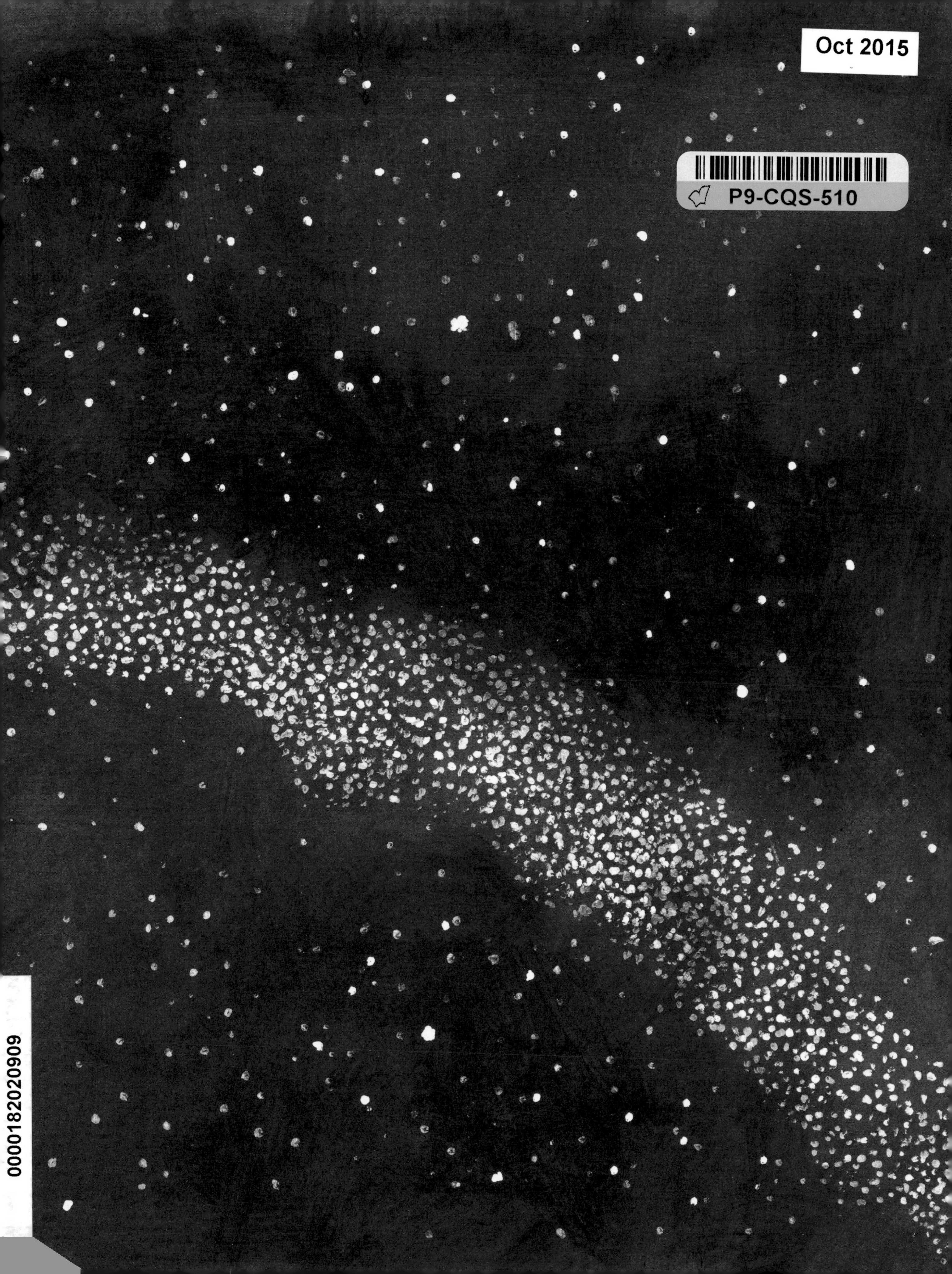

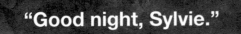

"Good night, Sylvie."

For my dear uncle
Philip Leo Chornow
1924 – 2011

Little, Brown and Company

Hachette Book Group
1290 Avenue of the Americas, New York, NY 10104
Visit us at lb-kids.com

Little, Brown and Company is a division of Hachette Book Group, Inc.
The Little, Brown name and logo are trademarks of Hachette Book Group, Inc.

The publisher is not responsible for websites (or their content) that are not owned by the publisher.

First Edition: June 2015

Library of Congress Cataloging-in-Publication Data

Gerstein, Mordicai, author, illustrator.
The night world / by Mordicai Gerstein. — First edition.
pages cm
Summary: Sylvie the cat persuades her boy to go into the darkness very late at night, where they are greeted by the shadows of roses and other flowers, and by nocturnal animals who whisper, "it's almost here."
ISBN 978-0-316-18822-7 (hc)
[1. Night—Fiction. 2. Sun—Rising and setting—Fiction. 3. Colors—Fiction. 4. Cats—Fiction. 5. Animals—Fiction.] I. Title.
PZ7.G325Nig 2015
[E]—dc23
2014006903

10 9 8 7 6 5 4 3 2 1

IM

Printed in China

THE
NIGHT WORLD

Mordicai Gerstein

Ⓛ Ⓑ

Little, Brown and Company

New York   Boston

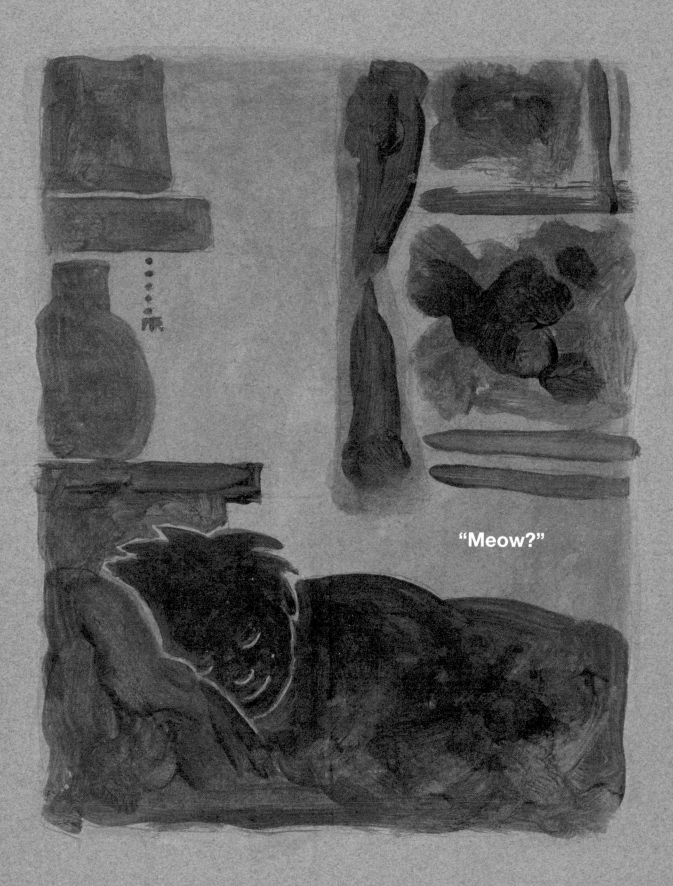

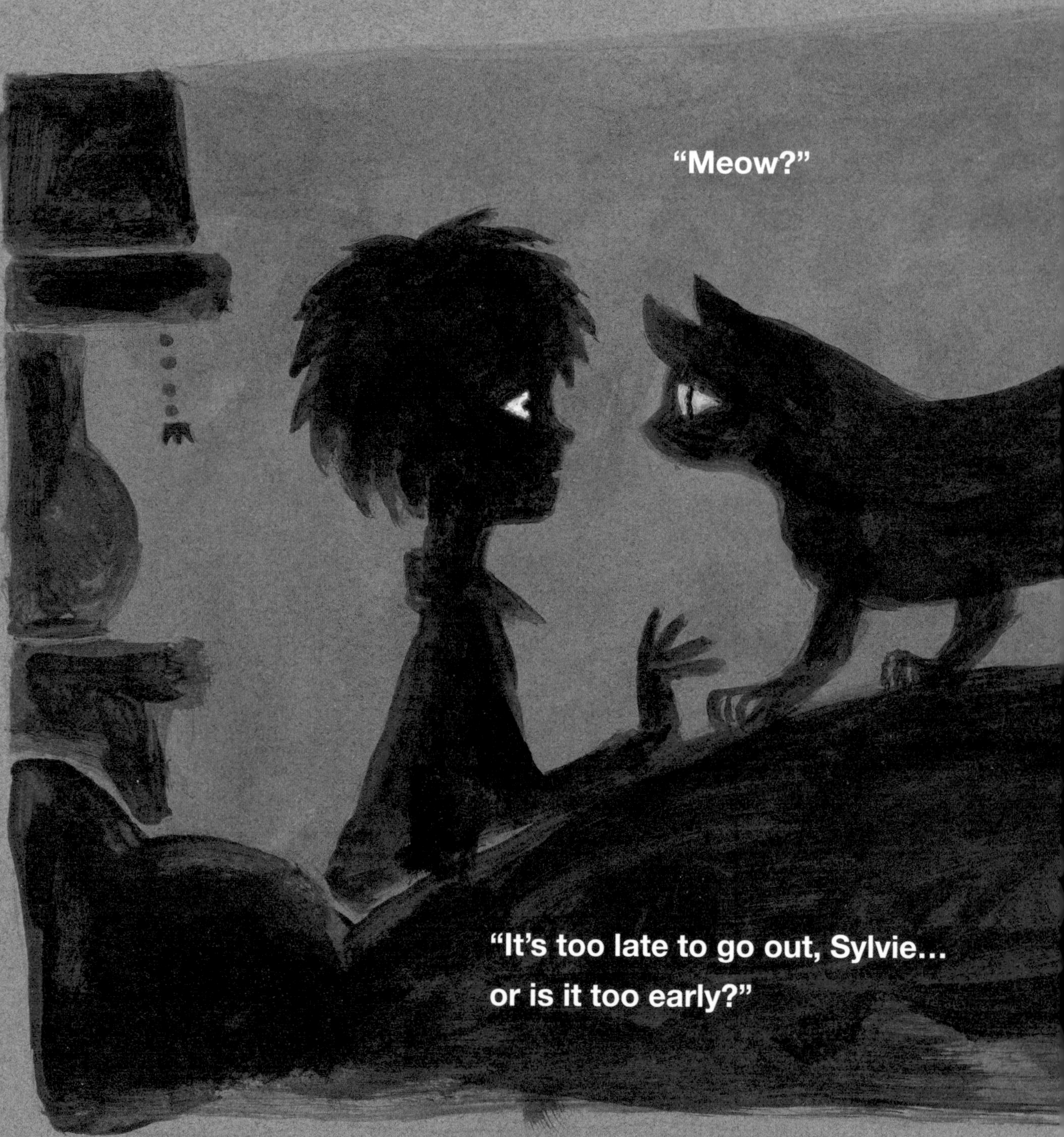

"Meow?"

"It's too late to go out, Sylvie…
or is it too early?"

Everyone is sleeping,
even the goldfish.

Everyone except for Sylvie and me.

Is this our house? In the dark,
it seems a different place.

"Me-out!" says Sylvie. "It's coming."

"What's coming?"

"It's almost here," she says. "Hurry!"

The grass is wet with dew.
The air is warm and sweet.
The dark is soft and comfortable.

This is the night world.
There are shadows everywhere.

Are these shadows roses?

Are those lilies and sunflowers?
Where are their colors?

That shadow is a deer.
Is this one a rabbit?

A porcupine looks up and
whispers, "It's almost here."

"It's coming," murmur all the animals. "It's almost here!"

Then a robin says,
"It's on its way!"
Now another, farther off.
"Here it comes!"

"It's almost here," says a chickadee.
"It's almost here!"
Now birds, near and far—
each in its own language:
"It's on its way!"

"Look!" says Sylvie.
"Look! Look!"
sing all the birds.
Suddenly, all is still.

Through the leaves of the trees,
there is a glow.

Here and there, shadows start to slip away.

"Where's everyone going?" I ask.

"This is our bedtime," says the porcupine.

"Sweet dreams!" say I.

The glow flares above the trees.
Clouds turn pink and orange.

The grass turns green.
The roses turn pink and red.
The lilies and sunflowers turn yellow.
"It's here!" says Sylvie.

And the great, glowing golden disk of the sun bursts from the tops of the trees.

"Good morning, sun," says Sylvie.
"Good morning!" sing all the birds.
"It's going to be a beautiful day!"
I sing, too. "Good morning, sun!"

"And good morning to you, Sylvie."

"Meow," says Sylvie.

From the house, I hear yawns.
Everyone is waking up.
"Good morning, everyone!
It's going to be a beautiful day!"

AUTHOR'S NOTE

One night when I was four,
I awoke in the dark. I called to my father:
"Daddy, I have to pee!" He carried me to the bathroom,
but on the way back to bed, we went through the kitchen.
Out the window, where the familiar backyard should have been, I saw a place
I'd never seen before, full of dark shadows and strange silvery shapes.

"Where's the backyard?" I asked.

"You're looking at it," said my father.

"No," I said. "That's the night world. It's not for me."
I knew I would go out and explore it when I was a grown-up, but not now.

The next morning, my backyard had returned to where it had always been.

I've also been a great watcher of sunrises;
to me, they are like watching the creation of the world.

Mordicai Gerstein

The illustrations for this book were done in acrylics, pen and ink, and colored pencil on Strathmore gray Artagain paper. The text and display type were set in Helvetica Neue 75 Bold.

This book was edited by Alvina Ling and designed by Saho Fujii. The production was supervised by Erika Schwartz, and the production editor was Wendy Dopkin.